Garry Chapman

eXtreme SPORTS

MOUNTAINS

SUMMIT FREE PUBLIC LIBRARY
75 MAPLE STREET
SUMMIT, NJ 07901

WARNING:

Extreme sports can be very dangerous. Mishaps can result in death or serious injury.
Seek expert advice before attempting any of the stunts you read about in this book.

This book is for Rob, Sally, Renee and Nicole Chambers.

This edition first published in 2002 in the United States of America by Chelsea House Publishers, a subsidiary of Haights Cross Communications.

Reprinted 2002

All rights reserved. No part of this publication may be reproduced or transmitted in any form or by any means without the written permission of the publisher.

Chelsea House Publishers
1974 Sproul Road, Suite 400
Broomall, PA 19008-0914

The Chelsea House world wide web address is www.chelseahouse.com

Library of Congress Cataloging-in-Publication Data Applied for.

ISBN 0-7910-6610-X

First published in 2001 by
Macmillan Education Australia Pty Ltd
627 Chapel Street, South Yarra, Australia, 3141

Copyright © Garry Chapman 2001

Edited by Renée Otmar, Otmar Miller Consultancy Pty Ltd
Text design by if design
Cover design by if design
Printed in China

Acknowledgements
The author and the publisher are grateful to the following for permission to reproduce copyright material:

Cover photo of rock-climber courtesy of Sport. The Library/Matt Darby.

AAP Image, p. 17; Allsport/Aris Mihich, p. 15; Allsport/Graham Chadwick, p. 16; Allsport/Graham Chadwick, pp. 27 (insert), 29; Allsport/Nathan Bilow, p. 14; Allsport/Vandystadt, p. 9; Austral, p. 28; Australian Picture Library/Corbis, pp. 6, 7, 19 (top); Australian Picture Library/UPI/Bettmann, p. 5; Getty Images, pp. 13, 24–25 (insert); PhotoDisc, pp. 21, 30; Sport. The Library, p. 20; Sport. The Library/Charlie Borland, pp. 26–27; Sport. The Library/Chuck Solomon, p. 10; Sport. The Library/Eric Reynolds, p. 11; Sport. The Library/ G. Schiffmann, p. 12; Sport. The Library/Matt Darby, pp. 4, 22; Sport. The Library/Ryan Gormly. pp. 8, 18–19; Sport. The Library/Simon Carter, p. 23.

While every care has been taken to trace and acknowledge copyright the publishers tender their apologies for any accidental infringement where copyright has proved untraceable.

DISCLAIMER
The extreme sports described in this book are potentially dangerous, and can result in death or serious injury if attempted by inexperienced persons. The author and the publishers wish to advise readers that they take no responsibility for any mishaps that may occur as the result of persons attempting to perform the activities described in this book.

3 9547 00289 9297

Contents

Home of the gods

Since time began, mountains have filled humans with a sense of mystery and wonder. For many of the world's peoples, mountains are holy places.

The summit of Mount Olympus was the home of Zeus, the most powerful of all ancient Greek gods. Moses ascended Mount Sinai to receive the Ten Commandments. *Chomolungma*, the name given by the people of Tibet to Mount Everest, means 'Goddess, Mother of the Earth'. Devotees of the world's major religions, Christians, Moslems, Buddhists and Hindus, make pilgrimages to sacred shrines on holy mountains.

Life above sea level

Mountains dominate the horizon for millions of people around the globe. For some, their steep slopes are home. It is estimated that about ten percent of all people on Earth live at an **altitude** greater than 1,000 meters (3,280 feet) above sea level. The mountains provide them with shelter, food, fuel and a livelihood.

Winter on the snowfields

For many people, mountains are areas for recreation. City dwellers flock to mountain resorts in winter to enjoy the annual ski season.

Summer in the mountains

In warmer weather, **trekkers** visit the mountains to explore natural places and to fill their lungs with fresh air. They slip on hiking boots and backpacks, and trek along winding rocky trails. Others like to take it easy in the mountains. They drive or ride in cable cars to scenic lookouts, and marvel at the breathtaking panoramic views that often extend to the distant ocean.

The rugged terrain of Mount Everest, Nepal

TAKING MOUNTAIN SPORTS TO EXTREMES

Sir Edmund Hillary (right) and Tenzing Norgay (left) conquered Mount Everest in 1953.

GLOSSARY

altitude – height above sea level

trekkers – people who hike through difficult terrain

terrain – the natural features of the land; the ground

route – the path taken up a rock face by a climber; each route is given a grade, determined by its level of difficulty

adventure racing – a long-distance wilderness race for teams, lasting several days and involving a number of different sporting disciplines

trail running – the sport of running along steep mountain trails

Trekking

Trekkers often gain as much pleasure from the beauty of their surroundings as they do from the vigorous exercise. Some push themselves even harder by trekking or running to extreme places, braving adverse weather and hostile **terrain** in order to reach their goal.

Mountaineering

Mountaineers seek the challenge of climbing high mountains. When George Mallory was asked why he wanted to climb Mount Everest, the world's highest peak, he replied, 'Because it is there'. Mallory died just a short distance from the summit. Countless other brave mountaineers have lost their lives attempting similar climbs of Mount Everest. Sir Edmund Hillary and Tenzing Norgay eventually conquered it in 1953.

Rock climbing

Rock climbers prefer a different challenge. They like to tackle the ascent of a sheer rock face by the most difficult **route** they can imagine. The tougher the assignment, the more they like it. Some climb the same rock in many different ways.

Mountain biking

The popularity of mountain biking is growing rapidly. Today's mountain bikes are just as capable of climbing steep mountain trails as they are of absorbing the bone-shaking impact of rocky descents.

Adventure racing

Perhaps the toughest test of endurance in the mountains is **adventure racing**. Teams of athletes race each other over hundreds of miles of remote mountain terrain. Along the way they engage in a variety of sports, such as mountain biking, kayaking, **trail running** and climbing. Only the fittest complete the race. Mountain trails are becoming increasingly popular for recreation. Many organizations conduct educational campaigns to try to reduce the environmental wear and tear on the trails caused by hikers, trail runners and mountain bikers.

The World's Mountains

Mountains dominate

Mountains dominate the land surfaces of our planet. They tower above the landscape in mighty ranges, on all continents on Earth. Mountains can also be found in the oceans, rising steeply from the sea floor to form islands such as Hawaii and the Azores. In fact, the longest mountain range on Earth is the Mid-Atlantic Ridge, which stretches beneath the Atlantic Ocean, from the Arctic to the Antarctic.

How mountains are formed

Mountains are formed in a variety of ways. Some are created by the push and pull of the massive plates that form the Earth's crust. As recently as 50 million years ago, the plate bearing the land we now know as India collided with the Eurasian plate to its north, piling up the mighty mountain ranges of the Himalayas and the Tibetan Plateau. Other mountains are formed when molten rock breaks through weak areas in the plates and forms volcanoes. Many scholars define mountains as parts of the land that rise above 1,000 meters (3,280 feet) in height. Mountains are quite distinct from their surroundings.

Europe's high mountains

In Europe, the great mountain ranges include the Pyrenees (Spain and France), the Caucasus (Russia and Georgia) and the European Alps (Austria, Switzerland, France and Italy). All year round, the Alps attract extreme sports enthusiasts from near and far. Skiing, rock climbing and trekking are favorite pastimes in these mountains.

Asia's high mountains

The high mountains in Asia include the Himalayas (Nepal and China), the Karakoram (Pakistan, China and Tajikistan) and the Hindu Kush (Afghanistan). These mountains provide the extreme challenge for climbers, with many peaks towering more than 8,000 meters (26,250 feet) above sea level.

Low clouds drift below the snow-capped peak of Mount Kilimanjaro, Kenya. It is Africa's highest peak, and is comprised of two volcanic peaks: Kibo and Mawensi.

A satellite photo of two of the highest peaks in the Andes Mountains, Solimana and Nevado Coropuna.

The Americas' highest mountains

High mountain ranges stretch down the Pacific coast of the Americas. They extend from the Alaskan Range in North America to the Andes Mountains in South America. In between lie several other mighty ranges, including the Rocky Mountains and the Sierra Madre. The highest peaks of these mountain ranges are popular with climbers, while the foothills attract followers of a number of mountain sports.

Africa's highest mountains

From the Atlas Mountains in the north to the Drakensberg Range in the far south, the high peaks of the African continent provide adventurous climbers with constant challenge. Some of the most thrilling ascents have featured the snow-capped equatorial peaks of Mount Kenya and Kilimanjaro.

Xtreme Fact

Mauna Kea, on the island of Hawaii, is the world's highest mountain. It rises 10,205 meters (33,480 feet) above the Pacific Ocean floor. Only 4,205 meters (13,800 feet) are above sea level. In comparison, Mount Everest is 8,863 meters (29,080 feet) in height.

Australia's and New Zealand's highest mountains

The Great Dividing Range spans the east coast of Australia. Its highest peaks do not reach the heights of the great mountains elsewhere in the world. However, the mountains lie within easy range of the biggest cities, and attract many followers of mountain sports all year round. The Southern Alps of New Zealand provide opportunities to participate in many different sports, ranging from snow sports and ice climbing to rock climbing and trekking.

Antarctica's highest mountains

A small number of courageous mountaineers have tackled the lofty peaks of Antarctica. In 1908, Mount Erebus, an active volcano, was the first Antarctic mountain to be climbed when members of Ernest Shackleton's exploration party scaled it. Several other mountains have been conquered since, but the remoteness of Antarctica and the harsh climate will always make any form of mountain sport extremely difficult.

Gear Up for the Mountains

a waterproof backpack with padded harnesses is ideal for carrying gear.

protect skin and eyes from the sun

This mountaineer is prepared for the full range of weather conditions.

gaiter

dress in layers

boots should be lightweight and flexible

FOLLOW THE RULES

The clothing and equipment required for mountain recreational activities vary greatly from one sport to another. In general, however, a few common sense rules should be followed when preparing for a mountain adventure.

DRESS IN LAYERS

Most experienced mountain adventurers recommend dressing in layers. This allows for peeling off layers when warm, or adding layers if the temperature drops. In high altitudes thermal underwear can be worn for additional warmth. Clothing worn next to the skin should be breathable, allowing perspiration to be taken away from the body. Outer layers should be windproof and waterproof. Fabric technology has improved mountain wear in recent times. One innovation is the development of polar fleece, a lightweight material used to make warm, comfortable jackets. Another is the introduction of clothing with sun protection factor ratings.

PREPARE FOR CHANGEABLE WEATHER

Many mountain sports will take adventurers into remote wilderness regions. In such places, the weather can be quite unpredictable. Mountain slopes can experience the full range of weather conditions in a single day. A trek may begin in full sunshine but adventurers can find themselves caught out in a terrible storm just hours later.

WEAR MULTI-PURPOSE FOOTWEAR

Many mountain sports require boots that are lightweight and flexible. Multi-purpose, waterproof boots are suitable for a variety of activities, including hiking, mountain biking and scrambling over rocks. They can even be useful when crossing shallow mountain streams.

Xtreme Fact

Gaiters are waterproof devices that act as 'outer socks'. They cover the lower part of the leg and the upper half of the boot. They are effective in rugged terrain because they keep burrs, water, dirt, pebbles and snow out of the boots.

CHOOSE A SUITABLE BACKPACK

If planning to venture into the mountains for any length of time, a backpack will be needed to carry gear. There are many different backpack designs on the market, each serving its own purpose. When trekking into a region where rain or snow are likely to fall, a waterproof canvas backpack might be most suitable. If a tougher fabric is required a heavy synthetic construction might be chosen instead.

GLOSSARY

harness – a safety device to which a rope can be attached, worn around a climber's waist and thighs

STAY WARM AT NIGHT

Sleeping bags come in a variety of styles. They are made to suit the different climatic conditions that can be experienced in wilderness areas. Sleeping bags are graded according to the temperatures people have to withstand. Serious climbers are likely to find themselves spending nights on mountainsides in sub-zero conditions. A good quality sleeping mat should be used under the sleeping bag, in order to keep any ground moisture away from the body.

USE PADDED HARNESS STRAPS

When selecting a backpack consider the weight of the load to be carried. A heavy load should sit comfortably on the back and shoulders. Padded **harness** straps will help spread the load.

A tent is essential for overnight stays on mountains.

PACK A TENT FOR OVERNIGHT STAYS

If staying out overnight a tent and sleeping bag will be needed. Tents come in a variety of shapes and sizes. Most modern tent designs are windproof and waterproof. They are made from tough synthetic materials and can be assembled in a matter of moments. When packed, lightweight tents fold up tightly and can be carried easily when trekking.

Safety in the Mountains

Learn the basics of climbing in a safe environment, such as a climbing center, before you venture out into the mountains.

Prepare before you leave

There is an element of danger in all mountain adventures. In one year in United States National Parks, more than 7,000 people are rescued, and 25,000 require some form of emergency medical service. Many of these incidents can be avoided if people are prepared before they leave home.

Learn the basics first

Perhaps the best advice is to learn the basics of your sport in a safe environment before you attempt to use them in hazardous terrain. Practice your climbing techniques close to the ground or in an indoor climbing center before you attempt to scale a sheer cliff face. If you are mountain biking, learn your craft on moderate slopes before you begin hurtling downhill on steep rocky mountainsides.

Ensure you are fit and flexible

Keep in shape through a program of regular exercise. Extreme mountain sports usually require a great deal of energy as well as strength and flexibility. It is important to know your limitations before attempting any difficult or potentially dangerous maneuvers.

Check your equipment

No matter which mountain sport you try, it is essential to have your equipment checked regularly. Climbing ropes can fray. Mountain bike parts can fracture. A trained eye will spot any faulty equipment before it is too late. When you use faulty equipment in extreme sports, you risk serious injury, or even death.

Let others know of your plans

Before setting out on extended mountain adventures, you must research and plan your routes carefully in advance. Prepare the appropriate clothing and equipment for all possible weather conditions you may encounter. Before venturing into remote mountain terrain, inform friends or authorities of the route you plan to follow and the time you expect to return. If you are sensible enough to tell someone where you are going, there is a greater chance of being rescued if you become lost or injured.

Keep an eye on the weather

Monitor the weather before embarking on any extreme mountain sports. It is wise to have a safety plan in mind in case the weather suddenly turns nasty. In extreme weather conditions, it may be best to find shelter and remain there until the weather clears or help arrives.

Remember the essential items

A safety kit suitable for mountain adventure might comprise some of the following items:

- a trail map
- a compass or a hand-held **global positioning system device**. This may save your life if you get lost
- a bottle of water
- a supply of energy food — your body will burn up energy and dehydrate very quickly after strenuous exercise
- a small first aid kit may help you deal with any minor injuries.

GLOSSARY

global positioning system device – a navigation device that allows adventurers to determine their position on the Earth's surface to within a few feet

Go in a group

In most cases you should be accompanied by an experienced guide, a partner or a small group when you participate in any mountain sports. Think about joining a club that offers its members a program of well-organized, safe mountain sporting activities.

When participating in any mountain sports, it is best to go with a partner, guide or group. Plan ahead, and let others know of your plans, in case you need to be rescued.

Xtreme Fact

The Scottish Mountain Safety Group has developed an imaginary mountain range named Glen Arna. The Glen Arna study pack contains a series of practical problems, based on real life incidents from the files of the Mountain Rescue Services, to be solved at home. Working through these exercises will provide mountaineers with a better understanding of the skills required to survive in real mountains.

THE ULTIMATE TEST OF ENDURANCE

Modern athletes are always looking for new challenges. Adventure races emerged in the late 1980s as the ultimate test of endurance in extreme mountain sports. An adventure race involves teams of competitors striving to complete a difficult course over several hundred miles of rugged, mountainous terrain. Along the way they must perform a range of different sports. A typical race may, for example, include sections of kayaking, mountain biking, horse riding, climbing, abseiling and trail running.

Adventure racing may involve kayaking, mountain biking, horse riding, climbing, abseiling and trail running.

New challenges each day

Races take place over a period of several days. Each day presents new challenges as the terrain, the weather and the nature of the activity change. Some races allow the athletes to rest each evening. Others keep you moving for a full 24 punishing hours each day.

Mixed teams

Teams typically consist of four or five members, according to the race rules. Each team should contain members of both sexes. The entire team is disqualified if just one member fails to complete the course.

A team effort

As a competitor, you can only succeed if you do what is best for the team. At times you will be required to give assistance as the demands of the race take their toll on a teammate. This may mean simply offering a few words of encouragement, or it might involve carrying someone else's backpack for a stretch. During an exhausting race, when you are ready to drop and all willpower seems to have drained away, it is remarkable how the support of team members can keep you going.

ADVENTURE RACING

Xtreme Fact

New Zealand's annual Southern Traverse event requires teams to navigate through extreme mountain terrain at night, using only a map, a compass and an altimeter, often on unmarked trails.

GLOSSARY

checkpoint – a point on the course through which all competitors must pass

In adventure racing, competitors often have only a map and compass to help them find the best route to each official checkpoint.

Physical and mental toughness

In addition to teamwork, the attributes you need to be able to compete in adventure races include:

- a high skill level in all sporting disciplines of the race
- a high level of physical fitness
- mental toughness
- navigational skills
- problem-solving ability.

Remote locations

Adventure races often take place in some of the most remote and hostile mountain regions on Earth. Competitors usually find out their destination just prior to the beginning of the race, leaving them little time to plot a course. Team members must pass through each official **checkpoint** on the course, despite not always having a clear idea of how to get there.

Global positioning system devices

When teams venture into very remote areas, they often carry global positioning system devices with them. These devices accurately record their exact location to within a few feet, which is not only an advantage during the race but also vital should a rescue operation be required.

Team preparation

Two of the world's biggest annual adventure racing events are the Raid Gauloises and the Eco-Challenge. Teams form up to one year in advance of competing. The athletes spend the following 12 months gaining fitness and sharpening their skills in the individual sports they will perform. Teams also need this time to attract enough sponsorship money to be able to fund their very expensive training and competition requirements.

Adventure racing academy

In 1994, as a result of the increasing popularity of these events, the Presidio Adventure Racing Academy was formed in San Francisco, United States. The purpose of the academy is to prepare athletes for adventure racing.

The toughest race

The Raid Gauloises is the world's toughest adventure race. It began in 1989, when French journalist Gérard Fusil and his wife, Nelly Fusil-Martin, created an event to test the fitness, skills and endurance of participants against some of the most remote wilderness on Earth.

The first Raid Gauloises

The first race was held in New Zealand. Thirty-five teams competed over a course of more than 600 kilometers (373 miles) that took ten or more days to complete. During the first Raid, participants had to contend with raging rivers, high mountain peaks, thick rainforest and other varied terrain.

The team

Each Raid Gauloises team of five athletes contains at least one woman. Each team member must not only finish the race, but must also report to each checkpoint along the way. If just one team member fails to finish or report to a checkpoint, the entire team is disqualified. This places enormous pressure on the team to function as a unit, with members supporting each other through the toughest stages of the race.

Competitor endurance

Each competitor must race for days on end with no sleep, because every moment spent sleeping is a chance for opponents to get ahead. Competitors endure hunger, exhaustion, aching limbs and mental anguish. The athletes also suffer from temperature extremes. Competitors must take care to avoid both heat stroke and **hypothermia**. It is no surprise that less than a third of those who begin a Raid are usually still there at the finish.

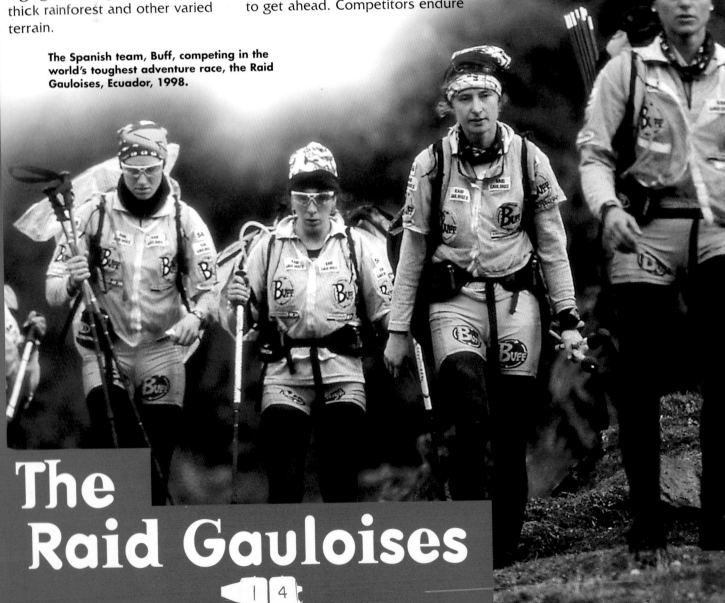

The Spanish team, Buff, competing in the world's toughest adventure race, the Raid Gauloises, Ecuador, 1998.

The Raid Gauloises

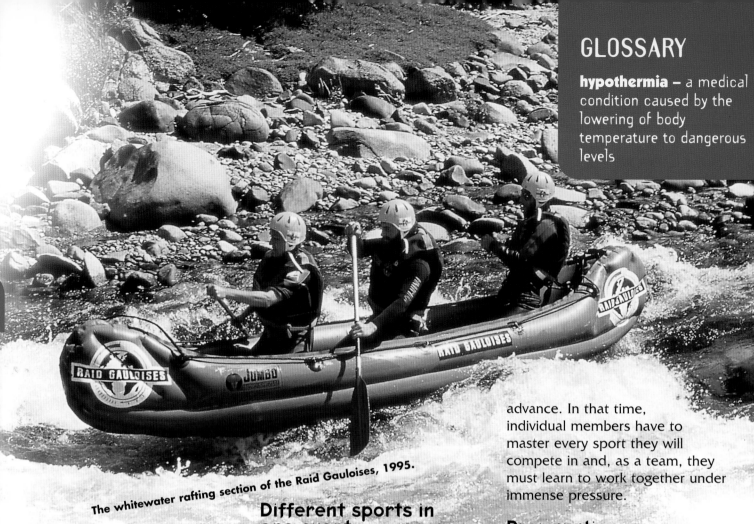

The whitewater rafting section of the Raid Gauloises, 1995.

GLOSSARY

hypothermia – a medical condition caused by the lowering of body temperature to dangerous levels

Event locations

The Raid Gauloises is held in a different country each year. Each location is well off the tourist trail, and the terrain is always extreme. Some of the wild places to have featured Raids include Madagascar, Patagonia, Borneo and Ecuador. Each course is unique, as the terrain varies greatly from one location to another, allowing race organizers to introduce new sports to each individual event.

Different sports in one event

The sports that make up a single Raid Gauloises are many and varied. They may include:

- mountaineering
- whitewater kayaking
- camel racing
- skydiving
- trail running
- mountain biking
- swimming rapids.

In order to prepare themselves for such an event, team members must begin training up to a year in advance. In that time, individual members have to master every sport they will compete in and, as a team, they must learn to work together under immense pressure.

Preparation

When teams arrive at the starting point on the day before the Raid Gauloises event, they learn the full details of the course. They must be prepared for anything, because it is only at this time that they learn of the hazards they may encounter along the way.

From sea to summit

A typical race was the ninth Raid, which took place in Ecuador, South America in October, 1998. Over a period of just ten days, competitors had to climb from sea level to above 6,000 meters (19,690 feet). The journey took them from the steamy Amazon rainforest to the icy glaciers of the Andes Mountains. Added to the challenges of the changing terrain was the difficulty in becoming accustomed to breathing at very high altitude. Only the toughest finished the race.

Xtreme Fact

The 1998 Ecuador race was the fifth Raid Gauloises for France's Sylvie Goyet. She trained on weekends by climbing to heights of 4,000 meters (13,125 feet), to the summits of peaks in the French Alps. The Ecuador race took Goyet above 6,000 meters (19,690 feet) to the summit of Antisana.

Environmental Awareness

In 1992, Mark Burnett, an ex-British Army paratrooper and former Raid Gauloises participant, established a new international adventure race. Burnett called his event the Eco-Challenge. One of the most important aims of this event is to raise environmental awareness. For each race, every team competing is required to take part in an environmental service project that will benefit the host country. Strict rules apply to the ways in which all competitors interact with the environment during the race.

The 1999 Eco-Challenge, held in Patagonia, Argentina. The British team, Hi-Tech, during the kayaking section.

WILDERNESS LOCATIONS

Eco-Challenge shares many similarities with Raid Gauloises. Annual races take place in exotic and remote wilderness locations. The landscapes must provide ample physical and mental challenges for some of the world's finest multi-skilled athletes. Recent event locations have included Utah in the United States, British Columbia in Canada, Australia, Morocco and Patagonia.

24 HOURS' NON-STOP RACING

The Eco-Challenge race usually takes a five-member mixed team between seven and ten days to complete. Teams race for 24 hours a day through all kinds of weather, using their best navigational and athletic skills to climb, kayak, ride or cycle between checkpoints.

Beast of the East

The Beast of the East, held in the rugged Allegheny Mountains of Virginia in the United States, is perhaps America's toughest adventure race. The six-day event can be entered by two - or four-person teams, or by individuals. Participants race over a course of around 500 kilometers (311 miles), climbing several high peaks and navigating whitewater canoes through a series of perilous rapids.

The Eco-Challenge and Other International Races

The Mild Seven Outdoor Quest

The Mild Seven Outdoor Quest (MSOQ) is another major international adventure race. The MSOQ event, which began in 1998, is a multi-sport **endurance race** undertaken in stages. It is similar to the Raid Gauloises, but there are a number of key differences:

- ☞ team members must complete each stage together
- ☞ teams do not have to navigate their own course between the checkpoints
- ☞ teams do not race 24 hours a day.

The route is clearly marked. Each stage of the race is timed separately and is added to the team's total to determine the overall winner. This gives athletes a chance to recover in the evening from each day's racing.

THE MSOQ 1999

The 1999 MSOQ event was held in the remote mountainous region of Yunnan Province in southern China. Participants competed in seven sports:

- ☞ running in single file along treacherously steep, rocky mountain trails
- ☞ mountain biking
- ☞ abseiling
- ☞ kayaking
- ☞ off-road inline skating
- ☞ traditional native craft paddling
- ☞ team biathlon.

GLOSSARY

endurance race – a race that lasts a long time and pushes competitors to their limits

TEAM BIATHLON

Team biathlon is an exhausting sport, requiring four athletes to ride and run alternatively, using only two bikes. Those on the bikes ride ahead of the runners, abandon the bikes midway along a section and run on. Their partners run to the bikes, climb on and cycle past their first teammates, who are now running. When the cyclists are far enough ahead, it is their turn to abandon the bikes for their teammates and run on again.

DISQUALIFIED TEAMS

MSOQ race organizers allow disqualified teams to continue running unofficially so that they too can experience the breathtakingly beautiful mountain scenery.

Xtreme Fact

Teams competing in the 1998 Eco-Challenge in Morocco rode mountain bikes, horses and camels. They paddled sea kayaks, trekked and climbed more than 480 kilometers (300 miles) through the High Atlas Mountains. The winners, Team Vail of the United States, finished in 6 days, 22 hours and 15 minutes — 7 hours ahead of the next team.

STUMPJUMPER

In the early 1980s, a company named Specialized released a product called the StumpJumper. It was the first mass-produced mountain bike available for sale to the public. The StumpJumper is great fun to ride.

A rugged off-road bike

A bike that was rugged enough to be taken off-road and ridden almost anywhere appealed to adventure seekers. Soon, a number of different makes and models became available. With each new bike released came improved design features. Knobbly, fat tires provided excellent grip and control for downhill riding. Handlebars were straightened for comfort. Saddles were broadened and padded to ease the impact of a jolting descent. Mountain bike sales soared.

Wilderness trails

Mountains provided the ideal environment for mountain biking. The scenery was breathtaking and the downhill runs provided plenty of thrills and spills. Soon, mountain wilderness trails, previously only available to hikers, were opened up for recreational riders.

Environmental awareness

Many hikers were angry about the invasion of their beloved trails by the mountain bikers. They complained that the bikes could cause damage to the environment and erode the trails. In response, mountain biking organizations formed which began to educate their members on the best ways to enjoy the sport without harming nature. Today, most mountain bikers are environmentally conscious.

Gears for climbing

The earliest mountain bikes were great for riding downhill, but not so good for climbing. Soon, complex gear systems were developed to make uphill riding easier. Riders found that, if they added bar ends, they could shift their weight forwards and upwards over the handlebars, which also improved climbing.

The mountain bike has features designed for riders seeking adventure in rugged mountains. Knobbly, fat tires provide grip and control, straight handlebars and padded saddles ease the impact of a jolting descent.

Mountain biking is a sport for all seasons.

Xtreme Fact

Australia's Cadel Evans won his second consecutive World Cup title at the under-23 championships, held in Sweden in 1999. In 1996, Evans was the youngest competitor in the field when the first-ever Olympic mountain bike event took place in Atlanta. He finished ninth.

improved technology

The latest mountain bikes come in a range of space-age materials, custom built for different purposes. Downhill bikes are fitted with fat tires and full suspension, to cushion what would otherwise be a bone-jarring ride. Cross country riders use lighter frames and narrower tires for speed on courses that are usually fairly smooth. General-purpose mountain bikes lie somewhere in between, offering riders great variety in frame design, gearing, suspension and pedals.

Hair-raising fun

State-of-the-art mountain bikes allow daredevil downhill riders to reach speeds in excess of 100 kilometers (62 miles) per hour. At this speed, trees, rocks and bends in the trail come at you very quickly, indeed. You need sharp wits and a great deal of courage as you hurtle down the winding trail on the very edge of control. It is quite hair-raising, but a lot of fun!

A sport for all seasons

One of the best features of mountain biking is that it is a year-round sport. In summer, many ski resorts remain open to mountain bikers. Some chairlifts even operate throughout the warmer months. The alpine high country can be quite spectacular at this time of year. Many of the steep ski runs provide the ideal venues for adrenaline-pumping, downhill riding. In winter, many of the trails are still quite suitable for riding.

Safety precautions

Downhill mountain biking can be quite a hazardous pursuit. When riding you must remain conscious of safety at all times. Your bike needs to be serviced regularly to ensure that it is always in peak condition. In potentially dangerous conditions, wear a helmet.

The start of the women's mountain bike race at the 1996 Olympics, held in Atlanta, USA.

CROSS COUNTRY RACING

Competitive mountain biking takes many forms. One of these is cross country mountain biking, which became an Olympic sport for the first time in Atlanta in 1996. The cross country race is a fast and furious two-and-a-half hour event. Competitors battle against each other and the clock to achieve the best overall finish. Up to 50 men and 30 women take part in events. The Atlanta Olympic races were held on a forested, 12-kilometer (7.5 mile) course, which was scattered with patches of granite rock and dotted with short and steep climbs and descents.

DOWNHILL RACING

Downhill racing pits riders against the clock as they hurtle down a steep, gated course at speeds in excess of 100 kilometers per hour. Many downhill courses are designed to challenge the skills of the very best riders, and crashes can be quite spectacular.

A typical downhill course

A typical downhill course may contain a number of different technical sections for riders to contend with. For example, riders may face a straight downhill, muddy stretch, a section peppered with large rocks, and a series of slippery switchbacks on a track strewn with smaller rocks and tree roots. Sometimes, straight sections of the track are linked by big jumps, which provide spectators with spectacular aerial action.

Dual downhill events

Dual downhill races usually provide plenty of thrills and spills. Riders battle against each other through a series of tight, slippery turns. There are often collisions on the turns as riders strive to gain an advantage over their opponents.

RACING UPHILL

Uphill mountain bike racing events are tough. Competitors race against the clock as they climb steep and often slippery slopes in order to finish at a higher altitude than they started at.

ENDURANCE EVENTS

A number of longer endurance events have been introduced to the mountain biking scene. One of these is the 24-hour mountain bike race. The aim is for teams or individual competitors to complete as many laps of a course as they can in the allotted time. A typical course is 12 to 16 kilometers (7.5 to 10 miles) in length. Riders face the usual difficulties of steep climbs, treacherous descents, narrow track and countless obstacles. In addition, they have to cope with fatigue, aching muscles, dehydration and lack of sleep. This demanding event requires supreme physical fitness and mental toughness from every participant.

Navigation and bush skills

Other endurance events combine mountain biking ability with navigation and bush skills. One such event is the two-day Gore-Tex Polaris Challenge. Teams of two riders have to ride long distances across terrain that is varied and often quite challenging, to reach a series of checkpoints. Points are gained along the way, and are tallied to determine the winning team.

CARRYING THE GEAR

Additional pressure on the riders comes from having to carry all the gear they will need to camp overnight. The responsibility for the gear is shared between the two team members, who use a combination of on- and off-bike bags to carry it. It is not easy trying to negotiate difficult terrain while carrying a tent, sleeping bags, a stove and enough food to last two days.

Xtreme Fact

Perhaps the world's toughest mountain bike race is Costa Rica's annual *La Ruta de los Conquistadores*. This race follows the route blazed by Spanish explorers in the 1560s, from the Pacific to the Caribbean coast. The race takes three days to complete, and takes competitors through steamy rainforest and volcanic regions.

ROCK CLIMBING

People have been climbing sheer rock faces for a long time. At first, rock climbing was a skill some people had to learn in order to survive. They may have climbed because it was a way to reach food. Perhaps they favored the honey from bees' hives, or the eggs from birds' nests perched on rocky cliffs. Another reason people may have climbed rocks was to reach high lookout posts. From there they could spot an advancing army and prepare for battle long before the enemy reached them.

Rock climbing as a sport

In the 18th century, people in Europe began rock climbing because they enjoyed the challenge it presented. Today, rock climbing is well established as a sport worldwide.

Courage and confidence

Rock climbing is definitely not a sport for the faint hearted. It requires physical fitness, flexibility and mental toughness. A climber must be able to confront fear head-on. There may be occasions when you are faced with a life-or-death decision on the rock face. The next move may be crucial. You will have to consider the options carefully, and you may have to plan the next five or six moves before releasing your grip. Once an action is decided upon, it must be followed through with precision and confidence. Rock climbing requires courage and patience, as well as skill.

Different routes

There may be many different routes on a single cliff face. Each one is given a grade according to its level of difficulty. A route is named by the person who first climbs it.

In traditional climbing, two climbers work together to scale a cliff face.

Holds

When planning a route up a cliff face, climbers seek holds for their hands or feet. Holds are small bumps, dents or cracks on the rock face where climbers can gain a grip. Some cracks are very thin. They may be just wide enough to wedge in a few fingers. Other cracks are much wider, and often go all the way to the top. Sometimes you can squeeze inside one of these 'chimneys' and press your back against one wall of the crack while you climb it with your hands and feet.

Traditional climbing

There are basically two forms of climbing: traditional climbing and sport climbing. In traditional climbing, two climbers work together to scale a cliff face. One climber, known as the lead, drives removable pegs or pitons securely into cracks in the rock. Metal safety devices called **karabiners** attach a rope to the **protection**, as this equipment is known. The second climber follows the lead up the rope and removes the protection.

The protection does not assist the climb in any way — it is used only for safety purposes. If you slip, the rope will halt your fall. Traditional climbing requires teamwork and a great deal of trust. You must focus on not only your own safety, but also on that of your partner.

GLOSSARY

karabiners – spring-loaded protection devices used by climbers to attach a rope to a harness or another rope

protection – the safety equipment used by climbers to hold them securely to the rock face

Sport climbing

Sport climbers use fixed protection. This is where bolts are permanently attached to the rock face. Sport climbers can devote all of their energy to the climb, because they do not have to place any protection on the rock.

Xtreme Fact

Bouldering is a very challenging form of rock climbing done close to the ground. It involves no equipment other than good shoes and a chalk bag, but it usually features an intense series of extremely difficult moves.

A lead climber (top) and her partner (bottom) climb Hanging Rock in Australia's Blue Mountains.

Climbing Techniques

Xtreme Fact
A good climber remains relaxed at all times, while maintaining tension on their body and legs. This keeps the body under control while the climber moves from one hold to another.

Popular climbing spots around the world feature many different types of rock. These include sandstone, basalt, dolerite, limestone, granite and quartzite. Each type of rock has different characteristics that affect the way it can be climbed. Start with the basics and gradually progress to more and more difficult climbs. As your climbing experience grows, so does your knowledge of different surfaces and the techniques needed to conquer them.

Staying in control
As an extreme climber, you must be in control of your body, mind and environment at all times. As well as understanding the properties of the rock and the capabilities of your equipment, you must be mentally tough and physically fit.

Being flexible and balanced
As a climber you must be very flexible. You will often find yourself in unstable positions, such as trying to balance on a single foothold. When this occurs, being flexible means you will be able to remain stable by leaning into the rock face and flagging out a leg in the opposite direction to your reach. Once balanced, you often require little more than finger strength to hold on.

Learning a range of climbing techniques
A variety of techniques are used during a climb. Sometimes a large crack presents a problem. It can be climbed by bridging, or stretching both hands and feet wide and pushing against the sides of the crack. If the crack is in the middle of a corner, try using a technique called laybacking. Reach up and pull your body up while you shuffle your feet, flat on the rock, upwards. If you cannot go up, try **traversing**. This is a technique for moving sideways across the cliff.

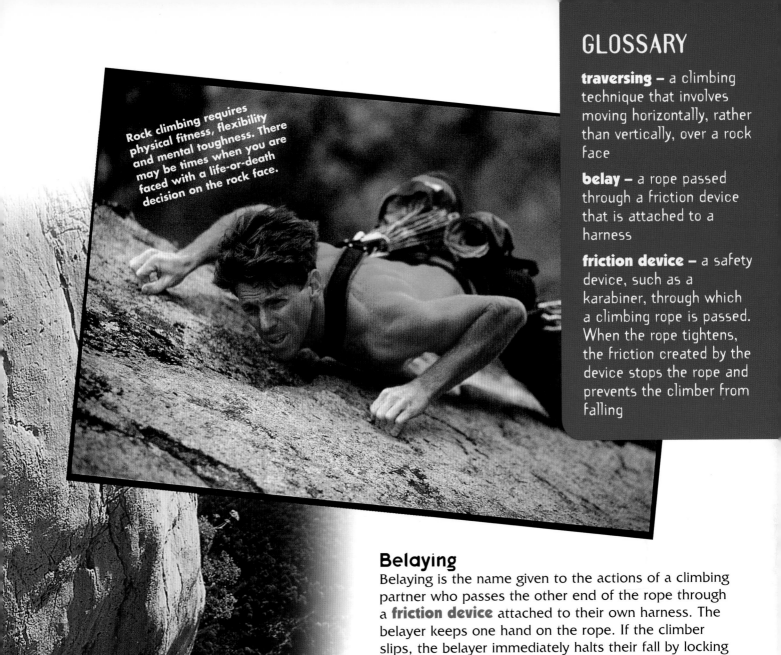

Rock climbing requires physical fitness, flexibility and mental toughness. There may be times when you are faced with a life-or-death decision on the rock face.

GLOSSARY

traversing – a climbing technique that involves moving horizontally, rather than vertically, over a rock face

belay – a rope passed through a friction device that is attached to a harness

friction device – a safety device, such as a karabiner, through which a climbing rope is passed. When the rope tightens, the friction created by the device stops the rope and prevents the climber from falling

Belaying

Belaying is the name given to the actions of a climbing partner who passes the other end of the rope through a **friction device** attached to their own harness. The belayer keeps one hand on the rope. If the climber slips, the belayer immediately halts their fall by locking off the rope with their brake hand.

Climbing without protection

The world's most extreme climbers tackle sheer cliff faces without the benefit of protection. They rely on shoes with sticky rubber soles that allow them to gain a firm grip on the rock surface. They also use powdered chalk, carried in a small bag tied around the waist, to keep their hands dry and able to grasp holds.

Feeling safe

Despite the obvious dangers of rock climbing, most of the world's top climbers usually feel quite secure on a cliff face. They rely heavily on their equipment to keep them safe. They wear a strong harness about their waist and thighs. A tough, lightweight nylon rope attaches to the **belay** loop on their harness.

Soloing

Climbing alone with no safety equipment is called 'soloing'. It is the most dangerous form of climbing, but probably also the most exciting! Many of the great solo climbs are courageous, death-defying efforts. When an exhausted soloist eventually reaches the top of a cliff and looks back to survey their successful route up the rock face, the satisfaction is immense.

ADVENTURE ON THE MOUNTAINS

Many people enjoy walking in the mountains. Some hikers make a day of it, setting out in the morning and returning in the late afternoon, after spending a pleasant day wandering along a wilderness trail. Those in search of greater adventure may extend their mountain jaunt to an overnight trek or one lasting several days. They may camp out in tents, or may shelter in trail huts during their **circuit** around the lower reaches of a tall peak or their traverse of a lofty ridge.

Favorite trekking regions

Some of the world's mountain locations that appeal to serious trekkers are:

- ☞ The Himalayas, in Nepal and northern India
- ☞ The Andes, in South America, especially the windy high peaks of Patagonia
- ☞ The Rocky Mountains of North America
- ☞ The mountains of Alaska
- ☞ Mauna Loa volcano on the island of Hawaii.

Off the beaten track

The most daring mountain trekkers are those who enjoy walking in extreme locations. Extreme hikers often venture into remote mountain regions in the far corners of the Earth. These are often places of rare beauty. You may find stunning landscapes, wondrous plants and animals, and native cultures that date back thousands of years.

Around each corner is a surprise

On an extreme trek, each twist in the trail is likely to provide something special — a new challenge, an unexpected surprise, a breathtaking view, a problem to be solved. Each memorable moment brings a new **adrenaline rush** for the hiker.

Extreme hikers often venture into the most remote mountain regions.

EXTREME HIKING

It will take your breath away

Extreme hiking often involves walking in hostile, rugged terrain. You may face long steep climbs along narrow, slippery trails, or obstacles that block your path and result in long detours. Your legs will ache and your back will strain with the weight of the load you are carrying. You will puff and pant heavily as the effort and the high altitude combine to take your breath away. There may be few places to stop and rest. One poor decision or one false step may result in death or serious injury. This element of risk is one of the reasons you are there.

Xtreme Fact

America's famous Appalachian Trail is about 3,475 kilometers (2,160 miles) long, and stretches from Georgia to Maine. Of the more than 3,000 hikers who set out to walk the trail each year, over mountains and through wilderness, only about 20 percent actually complete the journey.

GLOSSARY

circuit – a winding route which, when followed, will return the traveller to the original starting place

adrenaline rush – the special feeling that accompanies a thrilling experience

gruelling – exhausting; very difficult

You may return with every muscle aching and covered in scratches and bruises, but a hiking trip will be one of your most satisfying experiences.

Ready for all weather

Changeable weather is common in mountainous regions. Extreme hikers must be prepared for all weather conditions. Trekking in baking sunshine can bring on heat exhaustion or severe sunburn. A good supply of drinking water and sun protection is essential.

Rain can be hazardous

Persistent, heavy rain can turn the trail to mud and make rocky surfaces quite slippery and treacherous. Small streams can become raging torrents. Low mist can suddenly roll in and blanket everything in sight, restricting visibility to little more than a few feet ahead.

A satisfying experience

Extreme hiking can be a **gruelling** experience, but few who attempt it would be discouraged by that. You may return with every muscle aching, covered in scratches and bruises, yet you will most likely look back upon the journey as one of the most satisfying things you have ever done.

PUSHING THE LIMITS

A growing number of long distance runners are taking to the mountains. With hearts pounding, lungs gasping for air and leg muscles aching, trail runners push their bodies to the limit. They follow steep, uneven trails higher and higher up mountain sides, always scanning ahead for dangerous obstacles. A stumble on loose stones or an exposed tree root could be disastrous on a steep slope. As the altitude increases, the oxygen in the air becomes thinner, and every breath becomes difficult for an athlete. Trail running demands the highest levels of fitness and endurance.

Adjusting to high altitude

Extreme trail runners seek out the highest mountain trails in the world. Some muster the courage to compete in races such as the Mount Everest Marathon, which takes place every two years. Runners in this punishing event compete at 4,000 meters (13,125 feet) above sea level, at altitudes where acute mountain sickness can strike down anyone who has not **acclimatized** properly. Trail runners who run at very high altitudes usually need to spend days, or even weeks, at those altitudes, giving their bodies time to adjust to the thinner air.

Dressing for extremes of temperature

Extreme trail runners must be suitably clothed so that they have the freedom to run and yet be well prepared if the weather turns nasty. If the temperature suddenly drops high on a mountain trail, the unprepared runner risks hypothermia as the body's core temperature is dangerously lowered. On warmer days there is the danger of overheating. In order to guard against this, runners must drink plenty of fluid and avoid running during the hottest time of the day.

The Mount Everest Marathon demands that competitors push their bodies to the limit.

Extreme Trail Running

Trail running is a demanding sport. For safety reasons, members of a team run in single file.

GLOSSARY

acclimatized – having spent an appropriate amount of time at a given high altitude. This helps the body get used to the decreasing oxygen in the air, and will protect the climber from the harmful effects of acute mountain sickness

Xtreme Fact

Nepal's Mount Everest Marathon is run on rugged Himalayan mountain trails. It begins at an altitude of 5,180 meters (16,700 feet) and finishes at 3,440 meters (11,290 feet). The race includes two steep uphills. Following the 1999 event, the men's record stood at 3 hours and 56 minutes and the women's at 5 hours and 16 minutes.

Focusing on the trail ahead

Trail running is so demanding that runners rarely have the energy to carry on a conversation when running together. If runners pass each other going in opposite directions, eye contact is often the only form of communication which passes between them. All of their attention is usually focused on the trail ahead, trying to pick the best line to follow up the mountain and making sure they step over, rather than on, obstacles that lie in their path.

Enjoying breathtaking mountain views

Many extreme trail runners run in the mountains because they enjoy the environment as much as the physical challenge. It is not uncommon for runners to take a break during a run and soak in the wonders of nature that surround them. The majestic vista of snow-capped mountain peaks set against a blue sky, or the amazing sight of a mountain stream snaking its way through a deep rocky gorge, is enough to take the breath away. Runners who use the same trail throughout the year can watch the seasons come and go.

Being responsible

As the sport gains popularity and greater numbers of runners use the trails, the potential impact on the environment increases. Practicing responsible environmental habits means that the wear and tear on natural areas is kept to a minimum. Many trail running clubs around the world now play an active role in educating their members to be environmentally aware when they run.

Mountain Jargon

barn door
a situation where the foot and hand holds on one side of the body are lost during a climb

> "When I lost my holds I was left swinging like a barn door."

bomb
to ride down a trail at high speed on a mountain bike

> "He was eager to bomb the last section of the trail, but I took it easy."

clean
to ride a difficult section of trail on a mountain bike without any part of the body touching the ground

> "I've always wanted to be able to clean that last part of the trail."

dirt me
the command given to the belaying partner to lower a climber to the ground

> "I'd had enough climbing for one day and I asked her to dirt me."

endo
to hit a stationary object at high speed on a mountain bike and fly over the handlebars

> "I took the trail too fast, resulting in a nasty endo half way down the slope."

faceplant
a face-first collision with the ground

> "He took it a bit easier following the rather nasty faceplant he managed last time he rode this trail."

gearhead
someone who enjoys working on bikes; a mechanic

> "After that gearhead looked over my bike, it's been moving better than ever."

geek
an incompetent mountain biker

> "No geek should ever attempt to ride a trail that steep."

gnarly
awesome; really challenging

> "I've cleaned a couple of gnarly climbs in that area."

hammer
to go at something really hard

> "You may need to stand up on your pedals and hammer your bike to get up that slope."

roadie
a skilled cyclist who is not familiar with mountain biking techniques

> "He tried to handle the conditions like a roadie, and ended up in heaps of trouble."

thrutchy
a difficult climb requiring a great deal of strength

> "Faced with an overhang like that, I knew it was going to be a really thrutchy climb."

Glossary

acclimatize
to spend an appropriate amount of time at a given high altitude. This helps the body get used to the decreasing oxygen in the air, and protects the climber from the harmful effects of acute mountain sickness

adrenaline rush
the special feeling that accompanies a thrilling experience

adventure racing
a long-distance wilderness race for teams, lasting several days and involving a number of different sporting disciplines

altitude
height above sea level

belay
a rope passed through a friction device attached to a harness

checkpoint
a point on the course through which all race competitors must pass

circuit
a winding route which, when followed, will return the traveller to the original starting place

endurance race
a race that lasts a long time and pushes competitors to their limits

friction device
a safety device, such as a karabiner, through which a climbing rope is passed. When the rope tightens, the friction created by the device stops the rope and prevents the climber from falling

global positioning system device
a navigation device that allows adventurers to determine their position on the Earth's surface to within a few feet

gruelling
exhausting; very difficult

harness
a safety device to which a rope can be attached, worn around a climber's waist and thighs

hypothermia
a medical condition caused by the lowering of body temperature to dangerous levels

karabiner
a spring-loaded protection device used by climbers to attach a rope to a harness or another rope

protection
the safety equipment used by climbers to hold them securely to the rock face

route
the path taken up a rock face by a climber; each route is given a grade, determined by its level of difficulty

terrain
the natural features of the land; the ground

trail running
the sport of running along steep mountain trails

traversing
a climbing technique that involves moving horizontally, rather than vertically, over a rock face

trekker
a person who hikes through difficult terrain

Index

Chapman, Garry.
Mountains

J
796.52
CHA

SUMMIT FREE PUBLIC LIBRARY
75 MAPLE STREET
SUMMIT, NJ 07901

MAR   2007